A ROOKIE READER®

I AM

By Rita Milios

Illustrations by Clovis Martin

Prepared under the direction of Robert Hillerich, Ph.D.

CHILDRENS PRESS®
CHICAGO

Library of Congress Cataloging in Publication Data

Milios, Rita.
I am.

(A Rookie Reader)
Summary: Contrasts such differences as "I am big. You are small. I am short. You are tall."
[1. English language—Synonyms and antonyms—Fiction. 2. Stories in rhyme] I. Martin, Clovis, ill. II. Title. III. Series.
PZ8.3.M59Iac 1987 [E] 87-5163
ISBN 0-516-02081-1

Childrens Press, Chicago

Printed in the United States of America.
3 4 5 6 7 8 9 10 R 96 95 94 93 92 91 90

I am big.

You are small.

POTATOES

I am short.

You are tall.

I am up.

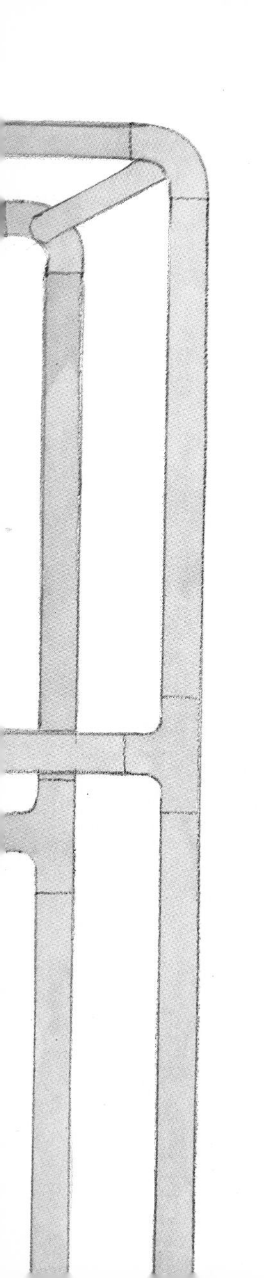

You are down.

10

I am black. You are white.

I can look. You can show.

I can stay.

You can go.

I am in.

You are out.

I can laugh.

You can shout.

I can say.

You can do.

I am one.

We are two.

We are many.

WORD LIST

am	in	show
are	laugh	small
big	look	stay
black	many	tall
can	one	two
do	out	up
down	say	we
go	short	white
I	shout	you

About the Author

Rita Milios lives in Toledo, Ohio with her husband and two grade-school children. She is a freelance writer and instructor in the Continuing Education department at Toldeo University. She has published numerous articles in magazines inçluding *McCall's*, *Lady's Circle*, and *The Writer*. She is currently working on her first adult book. Mrs. Milios is the author of *Sleeping and Dreaming* in the New True Book series. *I Am* is her first Rookie Reader.

About the Artist

Clovis Martin has enjoyed a varied career as an art teacher, art director, and freelance illustrator. He has designed and illustrated a variety of reading, educational, and other products for children. A graduate of The Cleveland Institute of Art, he resides with his wife and two children in Cleveland Heights, Ohio.